"Don't Let the Beasties

BY Julie Berry

ILLUSTRATED BY April Lee

J. PAUL GETTY MUSEUM, LOS ANGELES

scape This Book!"

"Godfrey, your father and I need extra help today.

After you milk the cow, please
feed the chickens,
spread the straw,
harvest the pears,
rake the leaves,
build the fire,
and light it for supper.

Now, don't make up stories and forget
to do your work again.

And don't disturb the artist who's here to paint
a Book of Beasts for the lady of the castle.

We're counting on you, Godfrey.
Can you remember all your chores this time?"

"Yes, Mother."

"So many beasts in one book!
But it hardly has any writing yet.
Just pictures.

Perhaps when it's finished,
this book will tell a heroic tale
of a long-ago knight who
battled dangerous beasts.

A mighty hero, a bold knight…
…why, Sir Godfrey the Glorious,
of course!"

Take care, young friend, if you
call the beasties by their names.
They may be in the mood
for mischief!

In which Godfrey invents a tale
and calls a beast by name.

"Listen, noble Doggy,
honorable Piggy, and
kittens of the castle,
and I'll tell you my tale.

Sir Godfrey wandered
into a wood one day.
He hadn't gone far
when a **LION** leaped out
from among the trees."

"The king of beasts
roared and showed its ferocious fangs.

But Sir Godfrey laughed in the face of fear.
With his bare hands he wrestled the lion to
the ground. It scampered off with its tail
between its legs."

In which the chickens are fed,
but not by Godfrey.

"Soon Sir Godfrey came to a clearing
where a UNICORN grazed in the sunlight.
When it saw the mighty Godfrey,
it pawed its hoofs and charged straight at him!

But Sir Godfrey the Greathearted stood firm.
He slipped a rope around the unicorn's neck,
fed it a pear, and brought it along on his journey."

In which an unseen newcomer
spreads the straw.

"Then a **GRIFFIN** came winging through the trees.
Half lion, half eagle, and all of it ferocious,
it lunged at the unicorn with claws outstretched.

'Steal my prize? My sword says otherwise!'
cried Sir Godfrey the Gallant. At the sight of his
trusty blade, the beast flapped away in terror."

"A shadow fell across the path. It was the
frightful **BONNACON**, most dreaded of all brutes
upon four legs! Its stench could knock him senseless!

The bonnacon raised its tail to blast the knight
with its odious wind. But Sir Godfrey the Grand
pushed the bonnacon into a running stream
to carry away the stink."

"At last, Godfrey came to a castle filled
with gems, pearls, and glittering heaps of gold.
When Sir Godfrey the Gleeful scooped the treasure
into his sack, a DRAGON soared from the topmost tower,
hissing and flapping its bat-like wings!"

In which Godfrey
remembers to build
the supper fire.

"But Sir Godfrey the Glorious scoffed at danger.
'Begone, vile snake!' he cried.
'This treasure is mine!' The horrid dragon filled its lungs to...

"Godfrey!"

In which the fire has been lit.

That's enough trouble for one day, beasties. Back into the book you go.

"I'm proud of you, Godfrey. I knew you could finish all your chores if you put your mind to it."

NOTE TO THE READER

By Larisa Grollemond and Elizabeth Nicholson

Imagine that you live in thirteenth-century England during a time we now call the medieval period, or the Middle Ages. You probably can't read. You never travel. You have very few sources of information, since photography, phones, and the Internet are hundreds of years in the future. In your medieval opinion, which of these animals is most likely to be real?

   1 – A huge beast with saggy gray skin, wiggly ears, and a horn on the end of its nose, stomping across the plains of distant Africa

   2 – A sea creature as long as two men, with a tusk on its forehead, lurking in the frosty depths under sheets of Arctic ice

   3 – A white horse with a spiral horn, wandering the forests of exotic India

Which did you choose?

1 – Rhinoceros

2 – Narwhal

3 – Unicorn

If you lived in medieval times and you heard stories about creatures you had never seen, from places you could never visit, you had no way of knowing whether such beasts were real or invented.

So, now you understand why people once believed in unicorns. And bonnacons. And griffins. And dragons.

BOOKS AND BEASTS

In this story, Godfrey finds a Book of Beasts, also called a bestiary. Full of drawings of different animals and descriptions of how they were thought to behave, bestiaries were one of the most popular types of books in the Middle Ages. All kinds of creatures both real and imaginary were included, from worms to birds to basilisks. Bestiaries also contained moral lessons and religious stories featuring animals, as well as pictures and tales that were lively and entertaining. You can see real medieval bestiaries in libraries and museums today.

Because printing hadn't been invented in Western Europe yet, books were made by hand, which took a long time—and a lot of different hands! A parchment maker made the pages out of animal skin; a scribe wrote all the words with feather quill and ink; an illuminator painted all of the pictures; and a bookbinder made the covers, usually with leather over wood boards. (In Godfrey's story, the book is bound into covers before being painted, but usually it was the other way around.) Since the process of making a book was very long and expensive, there were far fewer books in the Middle Ages than now, and these volumes were treasured by their owners. Like the illuminator in Godfrey's story, artists and makers of books often traveled from town to town, making books for wealthy individuals who could afford them.

LIFE IN AN ENGLISH CASTLE

A medieval castle was built to be home to a noble lord, who oversaw the surrounding land and its inhabitants. A castle was designed to be strong, to protect its occupants from attack. It usually had walls made of thick stone and was sometimes surrounded by a man-made body of water called a moat. Most often, a castle had a big building at its center with tall defensive walls all around it. The outdoor space in between the big building and the outer walls was called the bailey. The castle bailey was where a lot of the daily activity of the castle took place, and it usually contained kitchens, gardens, animal sheds, workshops, and a chapel.

The lord and lady were the castle's most important residents, but there were lots of other people who lived inside and also people who might visit on an average day. They included cooks, gardeners, horsemen, soldiers, servants, and peasant farmers who toiled on the lord's land. In this story, Godfrey's parents are peasant farmers who work for the lord of a castle. Farmers and their families lived on the land outside the castle walls, in small houses with dirt floors and straw roofs. They shared their (usually) one-room homes with their animals, including cows, sheep, and goats.

In the Middle Ages, peasant children had a lot of responsibility. They did not go to school and instead helped their parents with their daily tasks. A boy like Godfrey would probably not have learned to read or write, but like many medieval children, he would have done chores similar to the ones in this story: taking care of farm animals, assisting his family in the planting and harvesting of crops, and helping out around the house.

Of course, children were allowed to have fun sometimes. They played with simple, homemade toys and at games like tag and hopscotch. If traveling singers or musicians performed for the lord and lady of the castle, the local children were often allowed to watch. And, then as always, children loved listening to stories told aloud, like the one Godfrey makes up about a brave knight who battles ferocious beasts.

THE BESTIARY

The lion as the "king of beasts," the fox as a cunning trickster, the unicorn as a beautiful white horse with a long horn—these are concepts that came from the medieval bestiary and are still with us today. Bestiaries included illustrations of animals along with descriptions that mixed known facts, rumors, and Christian morals. Over time, the religious lessons faded away, and bestiary stories became the bases for scientific encyclopedias, studies of natural history and zoology, as well as works of fiction.

Don't Let the Beasties Escape This Book! was inspired by an exhibition at the J. Paul Getty Museum, Los Angeles, called Book of Beasts: The Bestiary in the Medieval World. For this special occasion, about one-third of all surviving medieval bestiaries were gathered from around the world, joining three examples in the Getty's own collection.

Below are a few images from actual Books of Beasts, along with typical legends and lore. Remember, not all of these animals are real, and not everything you read in a medieval bestiary is true!

LION

The lion is the king of all beasts. The roar of a lion makes all other animals shake in fear. Baby lions are born dead, and they are brought to life by the father lion's breath after three days. Lions always sleep with their eyes open. They are afraid of fire and the sight of a white rooster.

Bestiary, J. Paul Getty Museum, Los Angeles, Ms. Ludwig XV 3, fol. 68

CAT

Cats are useful creatures because they catch mice. They are swift and good-natured, but they will stop to rest in any comfortable spot they can find. Cats are excellent hunters because of their superior eyesight—they can see even in total darkness.

Bestiary, Bodleian Library, Oxford, Ms. Bodley 764, fol. 51

DOG

Dogs are unable to live separately from humans. They can cure their own wounds by licking them, and a dog tied to a person will cure internal wounds. A dog that crosses a hyena's shadow will lose its voice.

Aberdeen Bestiary, Aberdeen University Library, Aberdeen, Ms. 24, fol. 18

UNICORN

Fierce and fast, the unicorn can never be caught by hunters. But if a maiden sits in the forest alone, a unicorn will lay its head in her lap and fall asleep. The horn of a unicorn can detect poison, and if it is dipped in a poisonous drink, it will make the liquid safe again.

Aberdeen Bestiary, Aberdeen University Library, Aberdeen, Ms. 24, fol. 15

BONNACON

The bonnacon has the mane of a horse and the head and body of a bull. It has curly horns, which are useless for defense. The bonnacon attacks by expelling a fiery dung that can travel as far as two acres, burning anything it touches.

Bestiary of Ann Walshe, Kongelige Bibliothek, Copenhagen, Gl. kgl. S. 1633 4°, fol. 10v

GRIFFIN

With the body of a lion and the feathered wings and head of an eagle, the griffin is strong enough to carry a wild boar. Griffins live in mountains where gems and precious stones are found. They guard the gems and will not allow men to take them.

Worksop Bestiary, The Morgan Library and Museum, New York, MS M. 81, fol. 36v

DRAGON

The greatest of all the serpents, the dragon is one of the largest creatures on Earth. Dragons are the enemies of elephants, and they use their strong tails to catch elephants and other prey. When a dragon flies out of its cavern, the air around it glows.

Bestiary, The British Library, London, Harley Ms. 3244, fol. 59

Julie Berry is author of the 2017 Printz Honor novel *The Passion of Dolssa*, set in medieval France; the Carnegie Medal and Edgar Award shortlisted *All the Truth That's in Me*; humorous middle-grade novels including *The Emperor's Ostrich* and *The Scandalous Sisterhood of Prickwillow Place*; and the picture book *Long Ago on a Silent Night*.

April Lee is an illustrator, character animator, and 2D special-effects animator who works for several major television and film studios. Her animated e-book *The Dragon and the Pixies* earned honorable mentions at the London Book Festival and the Los Angeles Book Festival.

© 2019 J. Paul Getty Trust
Story text © Julie Berry

Published by the J. Paul Getty Museum,
    Los Angeles
Getty Publications
1200 Getty Center Drive, Suite 500
Los Angeles, California 90049-1682
http://www.getty.edu/publications

Elizabeth S. G. Nicholson, *Project Editor*
Elizabeth Morrison and Larisa Grollemond,
    Curatorial Advisers
Amanda Sparrow, *Copy Editor*
Jim Drobka, *Designer*
Michelle Deemer, *Production*
Kelly Peyton, *Image and Rights Acquisition*

Distributed in North America by ABRAMS,
    New York

Distributed outside North America by Yale
    University Press, London

Printed in China by Artron (AA18120222)
First printing by the J. Paul Getty Museum
    (16001)

Library of Congress
Cataloging-in-Publication Data

Names: Berry, Julie, 1974- author. | Lee, April,
    1982- illustrator.
Title: Don't let the beasties escape this book! / by
    Julie Berry ; illustrated by April Lee.
Other titles: Do not let the beasties escape this
    book!
Description: Los Angeles : J. Paul Getty
    Museum, [2019] | Summary: "A boy
    discovers a medieval Book of Beasts and uses
    it to invent a tale of heroic deeds. Each time
    he says the name of an animal, it magically
    emerges from the book, causing a day full of
    hilarity and mayhem at the castle"—Provided
    by publisher.
Identifiers: LCCN 2018045010 | ISBN
    9781947440043 (hardcover)
Subjects: LCSH: Animals, Mythica—Juvenile
    fiction. | CYAC: Animals, Mythical—Fiction.
    | LCGFT: Fantasy fiction.
Classification: LCC PZ7.B461747 Do 2019
    | DDC [E]—dc23 LC record available
    at https://lccn.loc.gov/2018045010

Bestiary illustration credits: Lion: J. Paul Getty
Museum; Cat: The Bodleian Libraries, University of Oxford; Dog and unicorn: © University
of Aberdeen; Griffin: The Morgan Library
and Museum, purchased by Pierpont Morgan
(1837–1913) in 1902; Bonnacon: Royal Danish
Library; Dragon: British Library / Granger